BENNY GATOR

Chrissie Kahan

Illustrations by Blueberry Illustrations

ISBN 10: 09979333-1-3
ISBN 13: 978-0-9979333-1-4

This book is dedicated to all the
kids out there who have been diagnosed
with anxiety. Never feel like your
disorder is a weakness. You just
see the world in a different way.
Remember, you are special, unique
and will go on to do great things!

Benny thought he was a dog like all the rest.
But he needed to use his mouth
for some reason when he was stressed.
If he started to feel anxious or upset in any way,
He would open his mouth like he
was an alligator until he felt unafraid.

Benny didn't know why

This was something he needed to do.
Each time he got nervous
He just had to open his mouth with his big teeth
and lick, pant, or chew.

And every time he opened his mouth like an alligator,
His owners would look at him and use his nickname to say,
"Benny Gator, Put Those Chompers Away!"

Benny was confused. He was a dog, not an alligator.

He wanted to bark
like all the rest.
But he had
so many thoughts
That made him
feel stressed.

When he heard the
garbage truck
He would freak out inside.
Thinking back to
when he was
an abandoned puppy,
This made him want to cry.

But he had a good home now.
Safe, where he was
loved and adored.
He didn't want to have
to use his mouth

To let out his
nervous yawn
and roar.

But the more he tried to control it

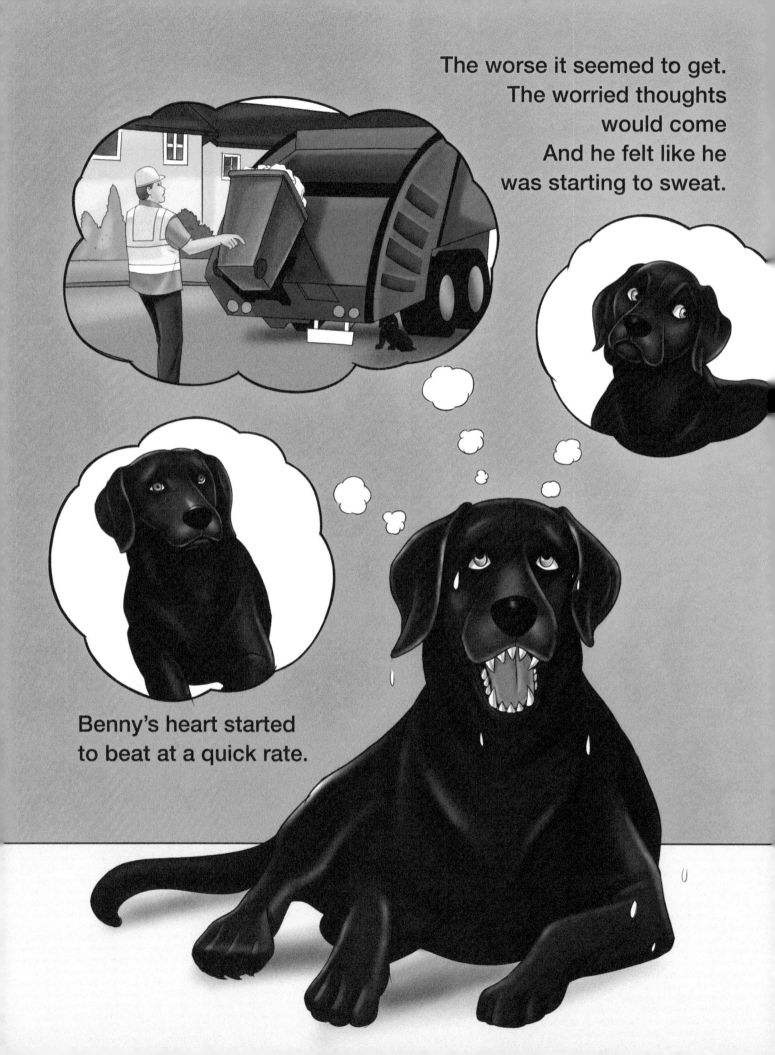

The worse it seemed to get.
The worried thoughts
would come
And he felt like he
was starting to sweat.

Benny's heart started
to beat at a quick rate.

His doggy mind racing all around.
He panted fast and loud, showing his large teeth
Until his tongue was close to the ground.

His owners petted him lovingly, Telling him everything was OK. Also saying, "Benny Gator Please Put Your Chompers Away."

Benny's owners
wanted to help
Him to not feel
so upset.
So they turned to
the best place
for research
The trusty Internet.

When they read
about anxiety,
It seemed that it was
something Benny had.
His worried thoughts
were not on purpose.
He didn't want to
be worried or sad.

Anxiety can lead to the following things:

PTSD

OCD

PHOBIAS

Anxiety

PTSD, OCD,
anxiety disorders,
and fears.

His owners read on,
just wanting a way
To relieve his worried
thoughts and doggy tears.

What they learned as they read on
Was that they needed to find
A way for Benny to know, understand, and share
What thoughts were on his mind.

Before his thoughts got
to the point

Where he would bite, pant, or chew
And his owners would have to say, "Benny Gator, Please Put Your Chompers Away."

They went to talk to a therapist

To learn about different ways
That Benny could control his thoughts
And have worry-free days.

Benny learned a lot
of different things
he could do
To help manage his
thoughts and anxiety.
The first was "self-talk"
which he learned is
The power of talking
back to his thoughts
to help his mind be free.

Benny would work
with his owners

Each time a thought came that would make him feel afraid.
He would let them know he was scared by putting out his paw.
His owners would pet him softly until
the worried thought started to fade.

See, Benny learned that
he could control

The thoughts that came into his mind, By talking back to those thoughts to stop them Or replacing them with happier thoughts he could find.

After his owners found a resource
From a website his therapist shared.
They used it to remind Benny
How to manage his anxiety and reduce being scared.

The saying goes just like this,
And Benny wanted you to know
In case you feel anxiety
And in your body it starts to show.

S cared?
What is happening in your body?

T houghts?
Think about your thoughts. How are they making you feel?

O ther helpful thoughts?
Think about something happier- a favorite place,
a happy memory, a good TV show, etc.

P raise yourself.
Say something good about yourself. You are amazing!

Benny had learned
that in his mind the
Thoughts were the key
To helping to control
and reduce
His anxiety.

Benny could now just be Benny
With no more need to bite, pant, or chew.
There was no more Benny Gator needed
Because his anxiety was something he could now get through.

Glossary

Anxiety: fear or nervousness about what might happen

Anxiety Disorder: a mental health disorder with feelings of worry, anxiety, or fear that are strong enough to interfere with your daily activities

OCD: Obsessive Compulsive Disorder: repeated thoughts that lead you to repeat certain behaviors

PTSD: Post Traumatic Stress Disorder: a mental condition that can affect someone who has had a very shocking or difficult experience

Phobias: an extremely strong dislike or fear of someone or something

About the Author

Chrissie Kahan has been an educator for thirteen years
and an elementary assistant principal for the past eight
years. This book was inspired by Chrissie's dog Ben who
was a rescue and truly suffers from anxiety. In her time
in education, Chrissie has worked with kids to help them
cope with disorders such as anxiety. Frustrated by the lack
of resources available, she wanted to create a fun, friendly,
yet meaningful book for kids and parents to have
in order to bring light to the topic of anxiety.

CPSIA information can be obtained
at www.ICGtesting.com
Printed in the USA
BVOW05*1000021117

499360BV00017B/342/P